A	B	C	D	E	F	G

	H	I	J	K	L	M	N

	O	P	Q	R	S	T	U

	V	W	X	Y	Z	

L.E.P.RECON

A	B	C	D	E	F	G

H	I	J	K	L	M	N

O	P	Q	R	S	T	U

V	W	X	Y	Z

L.E.P.RECON

Disney
ARTEMIS FOWL

GENIUS AT WORK
CODES, ACTIVITIES, PUZZLES, AND MORE

Manufactured in the United States of America
First Paperback Edition, June 2019

1 3 5 7 9 10 8 6 4 2

Library of Congress Control Number: 2019935578

FAC-029261-19130

ISBN 978-1-368-05238-2

disneybooks.com

Designed by DeMonico Design, Co.

A Mysterious SITUATION

Artemis Fowl's life is normal. Well, almost normal. He lives in a mansion and sometimes surfs home from school. And he has a Butler, who is actually a bodyguard, and some pretty cool gadgets and gear. But otherwise, pretty normal. Then his father, who he thought was off on another business trip somewhere in the world, is reported missing. And everything changes.

Now global authorities have launched a worldwide manhunt for his father, Artemis Fowl Sr. They suspect that he played a key part in some of the biggest unsolved robberies of the past decade.

When Artemis receives a call from a kidnapper demanding one ton of fairy gold for his father's safe return, he realizes there is more to the story than a simple disappearance. Turns out the fairies his father told him about might actually be real.

Now Artemis has to find a way to pay the kidnapper's ransom and try to piece together a series of mysterious clues to figure out what exactly happened to his father. Artemis will have to rely on his quick wits, old—and new—friends, and some pretty amazing gadgets to get his father back. But it doesn't matter what it takes; he will save him.

DECODING IN PROGRESS

WARNING: Some words in this book may appear in the Gnommish language. Use this Gnommish alphabet translator to decode when needed.

A	B	C	D	E	F	G	H	I	J	K	L	M

N	O	P	Q	R	S	T	U	V	W	X	Y	Z

FOWL PLAY SUSPECTED

Every time Artemis Fowl Sr. goes on a trip, he makes sure to send his son a **POSTCARD**. To find out where in the **WORLD** his father was seen last, Artemis needs to determine which **CITY** these last five postcards are from. He can do that by studying the stamp marking, called a frank. **HELP** him by numbering the pieces in the correct **ORDER**.

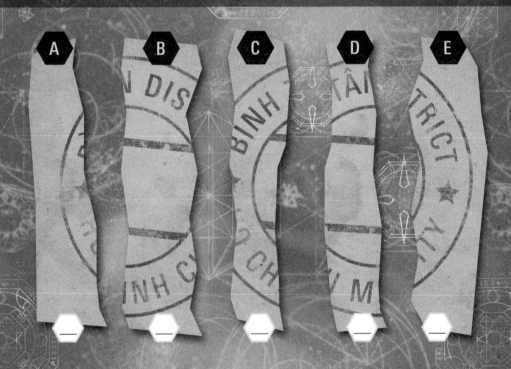

Then write out the name of the city here.

_ _ _ _ _ _ _ _ _ _ _ _ _ _ _ _ _,

_ _ _ _ _ _ _ _ _ _ _ _ _ _ _ _

MANOR MIX-UP

Artemis's family has lived in **FOWL MANOR** for generations. A computer **GLITCH** has caused this image of Fowl Manor to appear out of order. **PUT** the image in the correct order by **NUMBERING** the pieces 1 to 9.

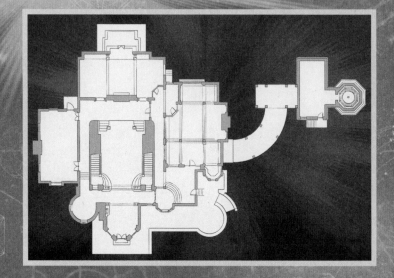

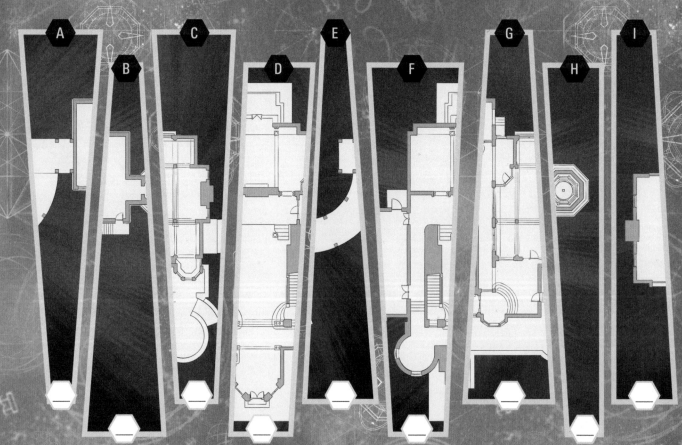

PUZZLING POSTCARDS

ARTEMIS notices something strange in the postcards his father sent him on his worldly **TRAVELS**. There appears to be a message. Can you **DECODE** it? **WRITE** the underlined word from each postcard above the **NUMBER** that matches the postcard it appears on to reveal the hidden **MESSAGE**.

4

Dear Artemis,
First of all, I hope you and your mother are doing well. I know it's been a while since we have been reunited, but please know that you are always with me <u>in</u> my heart. My work here is nearly done, and I plan to return home as soon as possible am certainly looking forward to be reunited.
All my Love,
Dad

2

Dear Artemis,
Well, today was quite an adventure. I bumped into 2

Artemis Fowl

Dear Artemis,
The weather here has been lovely although we are expecting rain in the coming days. Since I've arrived there hasn't been much <u>time</u> to explore, so I may need to extend my trip. Though I of course miss you and your mother, we will be reunited soon.
All my Love,
Dad

1

Artemis Fowl
Fowl Manor
Dublin, Ireland
United Kingdom

will turn out right in the end. It matters to <u>them</u> since they have spent a lot more time with it, but we will see!
All my Love,
Dad

5

it is hard to <u>believe</u> that it was only such a short time ago. Well, I've got to be going, but I promise to write soon!
All my Love,
Dad

3

Fowl Manor
Dublin, Ireland
United Kingdom

___ ___ ___ ___ ___
1   2   3   4   5

Character QUIZ

1
How do you feel about magic?

A. I absolutely, positively, 100 percent believe in magic.

B. Magic is overrated—unless you are talking about my magical art.

C. Magic is a headache. It causes more grief than it's worth.

D. I find the concept intriguing and want to learn more about it.

2
You've just chosen a new outfit. It's . . .

A. practical and easy to move in.

B. dark brown with many pockets—perfect for letting loose.

C. a well-fitted suit.

D. clean-cut with space for tech.

4
Your ideal Friday night would be spent . . .

A. solving crimes after a day of solving more crimes.

B. deceiving others.

C. spending time with family or training in the gym.

D. designing cool new tech.

Mostly **A**s
HOLLY SHORT

You're most like heroic Holly! You're strong, smart, and a good friend. You are a bit impulsive by nature and don't always follow the rules. But your heart is always in the right place, and you try to do what's right no matter the consequences.

 3

Your friends would say you are . . .

- **A** *not* a morning person.
- **B** an artist—all right, a *con* artist.
- **C** practical and reliable.
- **D** knowledgeable and determined.

Mostly **B**s
MULCH DIGGUMS

You're most like the sneaky—but misunderstood—Mulch! Sure, you might be criminally inclined, but you're always willing to help out . . . as long as there's a reward involved. Mulch's motto? Don't worry about what others think; live your life as you choose to.

Mostly **C**s
BUTLER

You're most like reliable Butler! Everyone's favorite practical friend, you are the first to take charge in a crisis and you give really good advice. Not much can shake you, unless, of course, you see a troll. Because those things are big. And ugly. Big and ugly for real.

5

Which quote do you most identify with?

- **A** "I heard you the first time."
- **B** "What's in it for me?"
- **C** "I believe I may still have the edge."
- **D** "I'm always right. Till I'm wrong, of course."

Mostly **D**s
ARTEMIS FOWL

You're most like intelligent Artemis! Confident and determined, you're usually the first person called on in class. You approach problems head-on and have an interest in all things tech. Despite your scientific passions, you are also open to the idea of magic and are able to see the more mysterious side of life.

UNCOVER
the DIFFERENCES

THE BOOKE OF THE PEOPLE is a text given to every magical creature on the day of their birth. It contains important and **ANCIENT** information about fairy laws, history, and magic. Below are two versions of *The Booke of the People*. **IDENTIFY** 10 differences found on their covers.

Answer on page 32

The **Booke** of the
PEOPLE

A. ⬡ ⬡ ⬡ ⬡ ⬡ ⬡ ⬡

___ ___ ___ ___ ___ ___ ___

B. ⬡ ⬡ ⬡ ⬡ ⬡ ⬡ ⬡ ⬡

___ ___ ___ ___ ___ ___ ___ ___

USE THE GNOMMISH ALPHABET TRANSLATOR ON PAGE 2.

C. ⬡ ⬡ ⬡ ⬡ ⬡

___ ___ ___ ___ ___

The Booke of the People is written in **GNOMMISH**. Using the translation guide provided, **DECODE** the words and then find them in the word **SEARCH** below. They can be horizontal, vertical, or diagonal.

D. ⬡ ⬡ ⬡ ⬡ ⬡ ⬡ ⬡ ⬡ ⬡   ⬡ ⬡ ⬡ ⬡

___ ___ ___ ___ ___ ___ ___ ___ ___   ___ ___ ___ ___

E. ⬡ ⬡ ⬡ ⬡ ⬡ ⬡

___ ___ ___ ___ ___ ___

F. ⬡ ⬡ ⬡ ⬡ ⬡

___ ___ ___ ___ ___

G. ⬡ ⬡ ⬡ ⬡ ⬡ ⬡

___ ___ ___ ___ ___ ___

H. ⬡ ⬡ ⬡ ⬡ ⬡ ⬡ ⬡ ⬡ ⬡

___ ___ ___ ___ ___ ___ ___ ___ ___

I. ⬡ ⬡ ⬡ ⬡ ⬡ ⬡ ⬡ ⬡ ⬡

___ ___ ___ ___ ___ ___ ___ ___ ___

```
O D L J D D Q B U T L E R
U G O P W Q P A M R Q T M
X U V G J S U A C U L O S
I Z G N C I J Z L G N K N
P K F O Z Q M Z G I Q K C
C O M M A N D E R R O O T
F K D M J C O T K Z A O A
M H A I Y U U Y B O K F R
X V E S Y E L N U W N L T
Q Q K H N C W I S N Z M E
A O L R L O E O E F W V M
M U L C H O L L Y T A A I
J X Z F W H Q R S O V F S
```

Genius at WORK

Juliet, Butler's niece, and Artemis are putting their genius skills to the test by **CRACKING** the code to the **GNOMMISH** alphabet. Put your **GENIUS** skills to the test by **FINDING** these items in the image below:

A laptop   A white sneaker   A watch
A calculator   A blue sweater   A lamp

USE THE GNOMMISH ALPHABET TRANSLATOR ON PAGE 2.

BONUS CHALLENGE

For an extra challenge, decode this word and then find the item in the image.

_ _ _ _ _ _ _ _ _

Answers on page 32

TAKING **COMMAND**

As head of the **LOWER ELEMENTS POLICE** (L.E.P.), Commander Root demands respect and calls the shots. To find out her latest **ORDERS**, write every fourth letter that appears in the **SPIRAL** in the spaces below. **START** at the red triangle and move clockwise.

USE THE GNOMMISH ALPHABET TRANSLATOR ON PAGE 2.

_ _ _ _ _ _ _ _ _ _ _ _ _ _ _ _ _ _ _?
_ _ _ _ _ _ _ _ _ _, _ _ _ _ _ _ _ _ _ _ _ _! _ _!

LAVA CHUTES
to the SURFACE

A magical creature is loose in the world of the **MUD PEOPLE**, and Holly is being sent by her boss, **COMMANDER ROOT**, to identify it. To reach the surface from the Underground, Holly needs to hit at least four **MAGMA BLASTS**. **TRACE** her path to the surface, making sure to hit exactly **FOUR** magma blasts along the way.

FINISH

START

Answer on page 32

Winged & DANGEROUS

Once **HOLLY** reaches the surface, she uses a pair of **MECHANICAL WINGS** for her mission. Can you **FIND** the pair of **WINGS** that matches Holly's?

1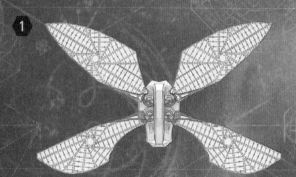

2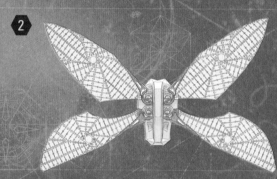

3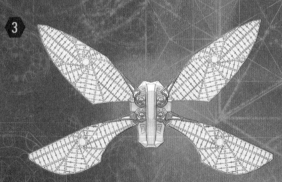

4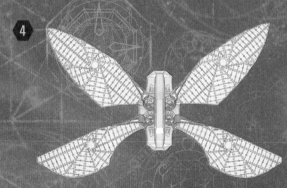

5

6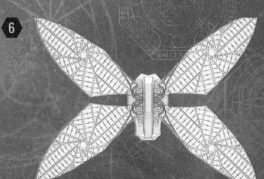

Answer on page 32

Mastermind MAZE

To **SPY** on the fairy world, Artemis and Butler thread a **MICROPHONE** down the trunk of an ancient oak tree. **FOLLOW** the microphone on its path as it leads to the **FAIRY** world.

START

FINISH

Answer on page 32

TECH IT OUT

ARTEMIS'S and HOLLY'S worlds contain some seriously AMAZING tech. DECODE the words below to find out the names of the DEVICES.

USE THE GNOMMISH ALPHABET TRANSLATOR ON PAGE 2.

A. _____ _____

B. _____ _____

C. _____ _____

D. _____ _____ _____

E. _____ _____ _____

F. _____ _____

Now create your own unique tech in the space below. What would it look like? What would it be called? What would its powers be?

Know Your NEUTRINO

The **NEUTRINO 2000** is an important piece of equipment for officers of the **L.E.P.** This nifty little **GADGET** may look harmless, but it packs a real punch. And if you need to catch your opponent off guard, the Neutrino can **TRANSFORM** into a bow or a sword right in the middle of the **ACTION**. Unfortunately, this particular Neutrino was struck by some powerful magic that sliced it into pieces! Put the pieces back in the correct order by numbering them 1 to 5.

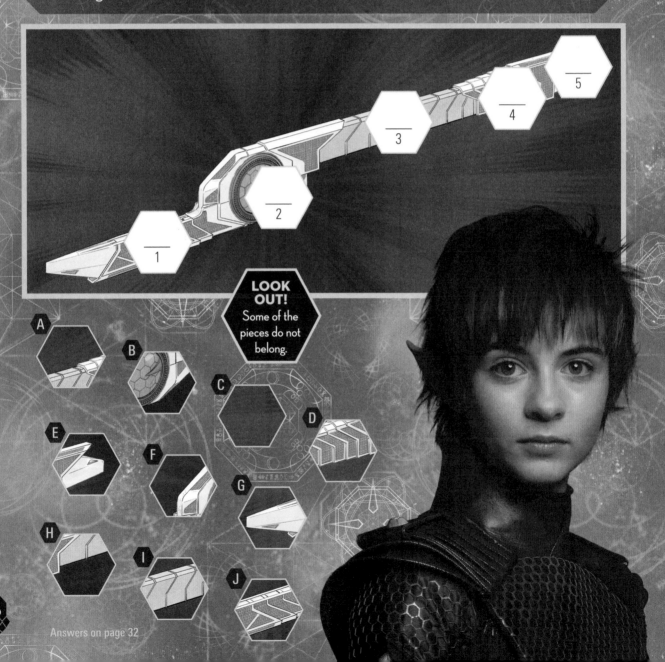

LOOK OUT!
Some of the pieces do not belong.

Answers on page 32

CRIMINAL MASTERMIND

FOWL PLAY SUSPECTED

	A	B	C	D	E	F	G

H	I	J	K	L	M	N

O	P	Q	R	S	T	U

V	W	X	Y	Z

L.E.P.RECON

© 2019 Disney

MORE THAN MEETS THE EYE

Artemis can block Holly's mesmerizing magic with his **SUNGLASSES**, but some parts are missing. Put his sunglasses back **TOGETHER** before Holly mesmerizes him.

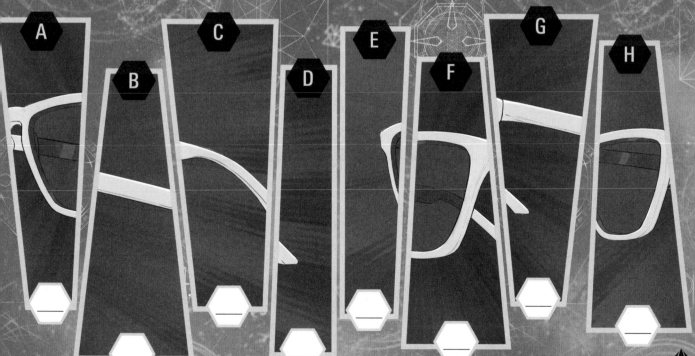

Answers on page 32

CRACK THE CODE

To **RESTORE** her magic supply, **HOLLY** must recite an incantation while planting an acorn in the ground. **DECODE** the incantation below to find out what she needs to say to restore her **MAGIC**.

USE THE GNOMMISH ALPHABET TRANSLATOR ON PAGE 2.

_ _ _ _ _ _ _ _ _   _ _ _ _ _ ,

_ _ _ _ _   _ _ _   _ _ _ _ .

_ _ _ _ _ _ _   _ _ _ _   _ _ _ _ _

_ _ _ _ _ _ _ _ _   _ _ _ _ _   _ _ _ _ _

_ _ _   _ _ _ _ _ _ _   _ _ _ _   _ _ _ _ _

_ _ _   _ _ _ _   _ _ _ _ _ _ .

Artful Acorns

Answer on page 32

As part of the **RITUAL** to restore her magic, Holly must select an acorn. Can you **FIND** the acorn that **MATCHES** hers?

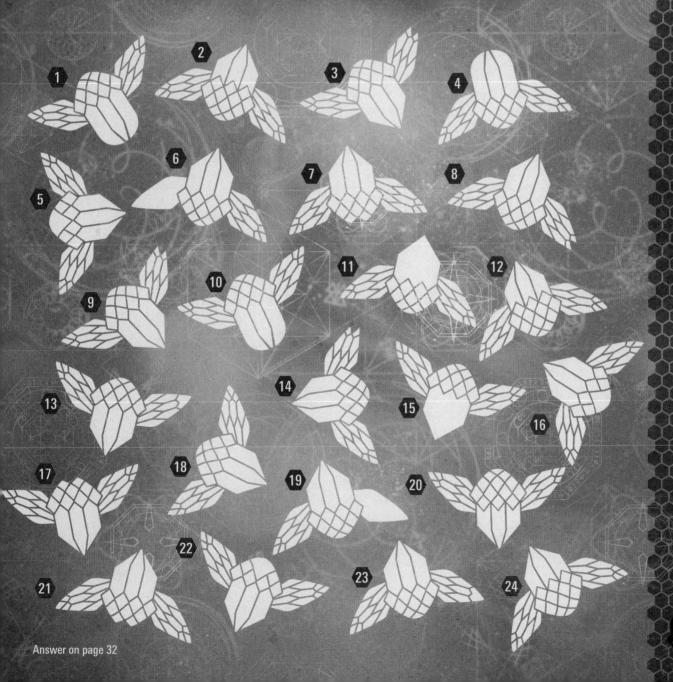

DIGGIN' IT

While he is not her first choice for **HELP**, Commander Root needs the con artist **MULCH DIGGUMS** to tunnel underneath Fowl Manor. **BUT** there's one problem: Mulch is allergic to limestone. If he eats too much, things can get a little . . . messy. **TRACE** the path that leads Mulch inside the **MANOR** without crossing more than two limestone clusters.

START

TIME FREEZE!

Commander Root has just placed a time freeze over Fowl Manor. Try to complete the maze in less than one minute!

Answer on page 32

GNOMMISH NUMBERS

How old is Commander Root? How long has the existence of **FAIRIES** been kept a **SECRET**? Use the Gnommish number decoder to reveal the answers to the **QUESTIONS** below.

CODE

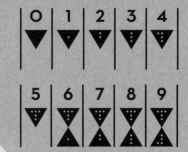

A. Commander Root is years old.

B. It has been days since Holly completed the ritual to restore her magic.

C. Fairies' existence has been a secret for  years.

Playful PATTERNS

Fill in the **MISSING** Gnommish numerals below by solving the **PATTERN**.

A.

B.

C.

Lost LETTERS

Some of the Gnommish letters in this sudoku puzzle have mysteriously **DISAPPEARED**! Complete the puzzle by **FILLING** in the blank spaces with these six **GNOMMISH** letters (, , , , ,). Each of these letters should appear only **ONCE** in each column, row, and rectangular section.

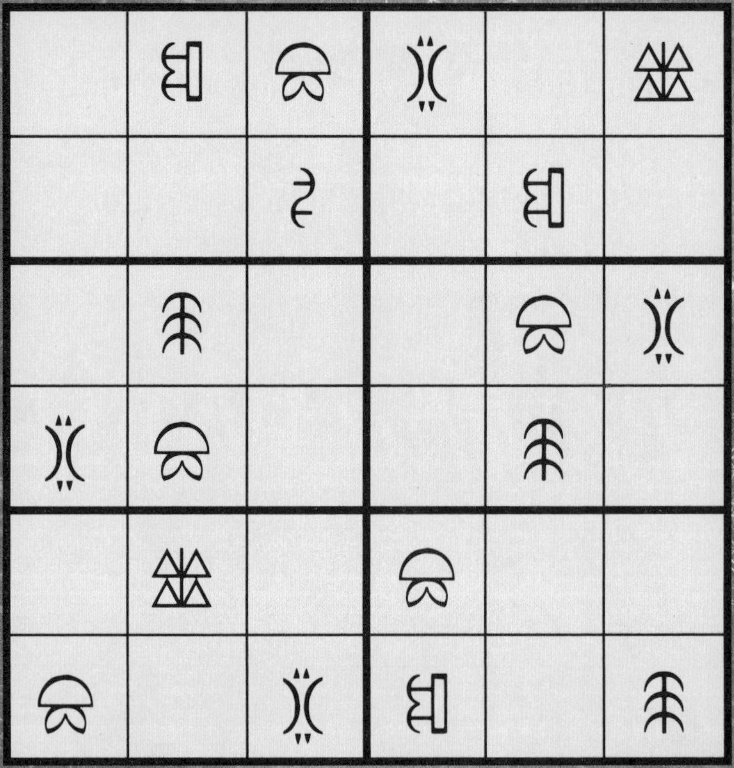

USE THE GNOMMISH ALPHABET TRANSLATOR ON PAGE 2.

Then translate the six Gnommish letters from the puzzle. Unscramble the letters to reveal a hidden word.

ORIGINAL:

_ _ _ _ _ _ _ S

TRANSLATION:

_ _ _ _ _ _ _ S

Answers on page 32

Play It SAFE

The **TXTL 5000** safe is one of the **TOUGHEST** safes on the market. The one inside Fowl Manor holds priceless **TREASURE**. See if you can **OPEN** the safe by figuring out the number pattern for each set of numbers. Then **FILL** in the correct digits!

A. What number should appear on the second dial?

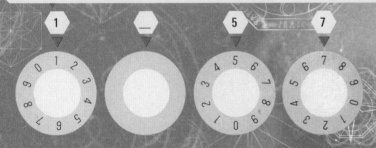

1   _   5   7

B. What number should appear on the third dial?

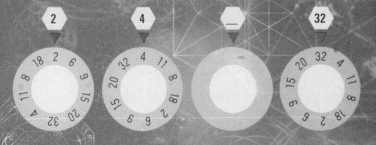

2   4   _   32

C. What number should appear on the third dial?

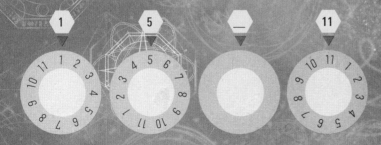

1   5   _   11

Answers on page 32

GO FOR GOLD

ARTEMIS needs to get his hands on one ton of fairy gold to PAY his father's ransom. Can you SPOT the fairy gold that is different from the others? ELIMINATE the matching pairs to uncover the AUTHENTIC fairy gold.

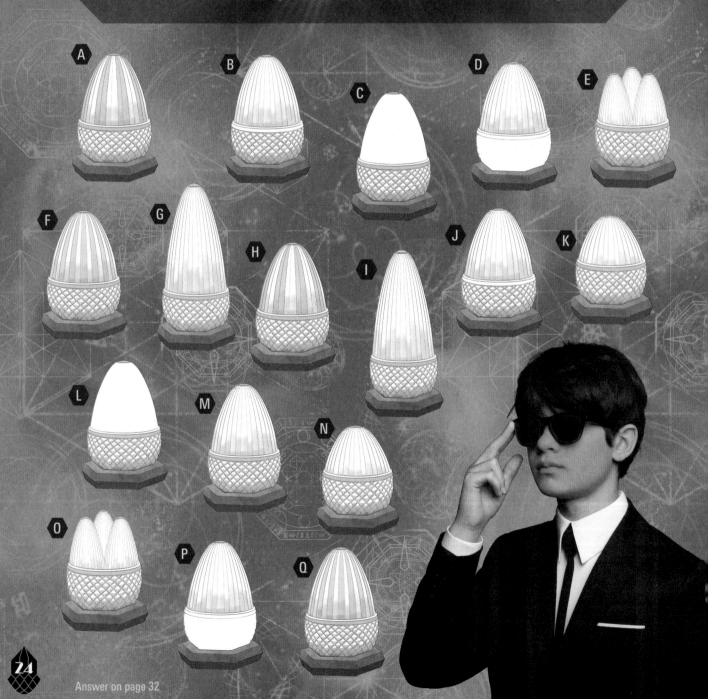

Answer on page 32

CRIMINAL MASTERMIND

Artemis wants to **RESCUE** his father from the terrible person—or fairy—who **KIDNAPPED** him. But to do that, Artemis needs to get his hands on some fairy gold and use it for his father's **RANSOM**. See if you can help him reach the **FAIRY GOLD** by **FOLLOWING** the instructions below.

To reach the fairy gold inside the wall of numbers you must follow these directions:

1. The number in the blue circle must be even.
2. The number in the green circle must contain double digits.
3. The number in the black circle is the sum of the first and second numbers.
4. The circles containing all three numbers must be connected.

98   3
0   45   18
11   16   21   5
18   [gold]   43
10   65   [gold]   13   26
29   [gold]   8
2   42   57   17
19   38   25
45   4

PLAY *by the* RULES

With a **FRIEND**, place two acorns or other small items, like beans or buttons, on the **START** space. The youngest player goes first. When it's your turn, **FLIP** a coin. Move **TWO** spaces forward for heads and **ONE** for tails. If you land on a space with writing, follow the instructions. The first player to reach the **FAIRY GOLD** wins!

Go back to START

Move ahead 3 spaces

Go to TIME FREEZE

TROLL TRAP!

SKIP 3 TURNS

START

Move ahead 1 space

FINISH

Go to
TIME FREEZE

Move back
2 spaces

Skip
1 turn

TIME FREEZE!

You must flip heads on your next turn to get
out. You have one try per turn.

When you flip heads place your piece back on
the board one space in front of the time freeze
space you last landed on. You may move your
piece on the next turn.

TROLL TAKEDOWN

Suits & SHADES

The **TROLL** has left a path of total destruction inside Fowl Manor. **COMMANDER ROOT** sends two advanced teams to survey the **DAMAGE**. Look at the picture for forty-five seconds. Then **TURN** to the next page and answer the **QUESTIONS** without looking back. You might surprise yourself!

QUIZ: *Suits* & SHADES

Now put your **MASTER MIND** to the test by answering the questions below.

1. Which characters were in the image?
   A. Artemis and Butler
   B. Holly and Artemis
   C. None

2. How many pillars were there?
   A. Four
   B. Six
   C. Eight

3. How many stairs were there?
   A. Twelve
   B. Five
   C. Eight

4. Were the L.E.P. officers wearing sunglasses?
   A. Yes
   B. No

5. How many L.E.P. officers were there?
   A. Zero
   B. Five
   C. Seven

6. What color were the L.E.P. officers' uniforms?
   A. Blue
   B. Green
   C. Black

7. Was there an animal in the picture?
   A. Yes
   B. No

8. Someone was looking out the window.
   A. True
   B. False

9. The door was open.
   A. True
   B. False

10. How many lights were on the chandelier?
   A. Eight
   B. Five
   C. Six

Answers on page 32

Mysterious MESSAGE

At the **TOP** of every page in this book, you will find **ONE** letter from the Gnommish alphabet. **WRITE** them in order below to reveal a **MYSTERIOUS** message.

__ __ __ __ __ __ __ __   __ __ __ __

__ __   __

__ __ __ __ __ __ __

__ __ __ __ __ __ __ __ __ __ __ .

USE THE GNOMMISH ALPHABET TRANSLATOR ON PAGE 2.

ANSWERS

3 FOWL PLAY SUSPECTED
a. 1, b. 4, c. 2, d. 3, e. 5
Bình Tân District, Ho Chi
Minh City

4 MANOR MIX-UP
I, F, D, G, C, E, A, B, H

5 PUZZLING POSTCARDS
Time 2 believe in them

8 UNCOVER THE DIFFERENCES

9 THE BOOKE OF THE PEOPLE
a. Butler b. Artemis c. Holly
d. Commander Root e. Juliet
f. Mulch g. Aculos
h. Gnommish i. Neutrino

10 GENIUS AT WORK

Bonus challenge: a painting

11 TAKING COMMAND
What are you waiting for?
This isn't a time freeze! Go!

12 LAVA CHUTES TO THE SURFACE

13 WINGED & DANGEROUS
3

14 MASTERMIND MAZE

15 TECH IT OUT
a. Neutrino sword
b. Holly's wings
c. Artemis's sunglasses
d. trouble kelp helmet
e. visor and binocular
f. flash cruiser

16 KNOW YOUR NEUTRINO
1. J, 2. B, 3. I, 4. D, 5. E

17 MORE THAN MEETS THE EYE
E, H, A, F, G, B, C, D

18 CRACK THE CODE
Moonlight shine,
moon be mine.
I thank the face
That lights this place
And brings the earth
Its holy grace.

19 ARTFUL ACORNS
18

20 DIGGIN' IT

21 GNOMMISH NUMBERS
a. 802 b. 160 c. 5,000

PLAYFUL PATTERNS
a. 4 b. 6 c. 8

22 LOST LETTERS

Artemis

23 PLAY IT SAFE
3, 8, 6

24 GO FOR GOLD
M

25 CRIMINAL MASTERMIND
4, 38, 42

30 QUIZ: SUITS & SHADES
1. c, 2. b, 3. c, 4. a, 5. c,
6. b, 7. b, 8. b, 9. a, 10. a

31 MYSTERIOUS MESSAGE
Artemis Fowl is a
criminal mastermind.

DIGGIN' IT

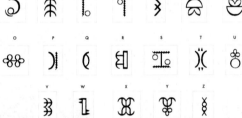

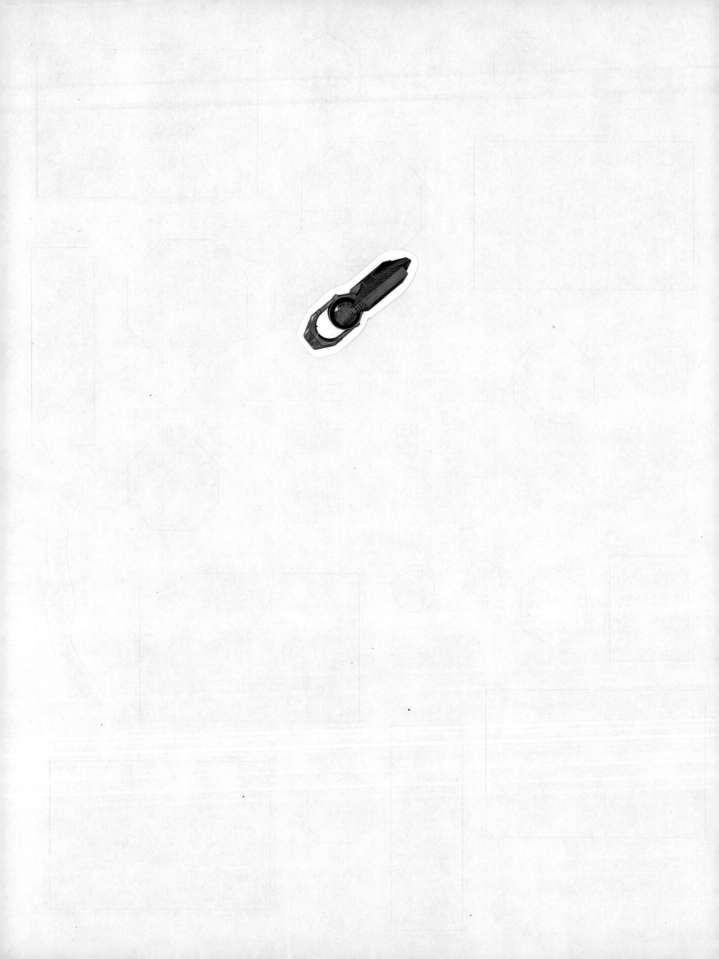

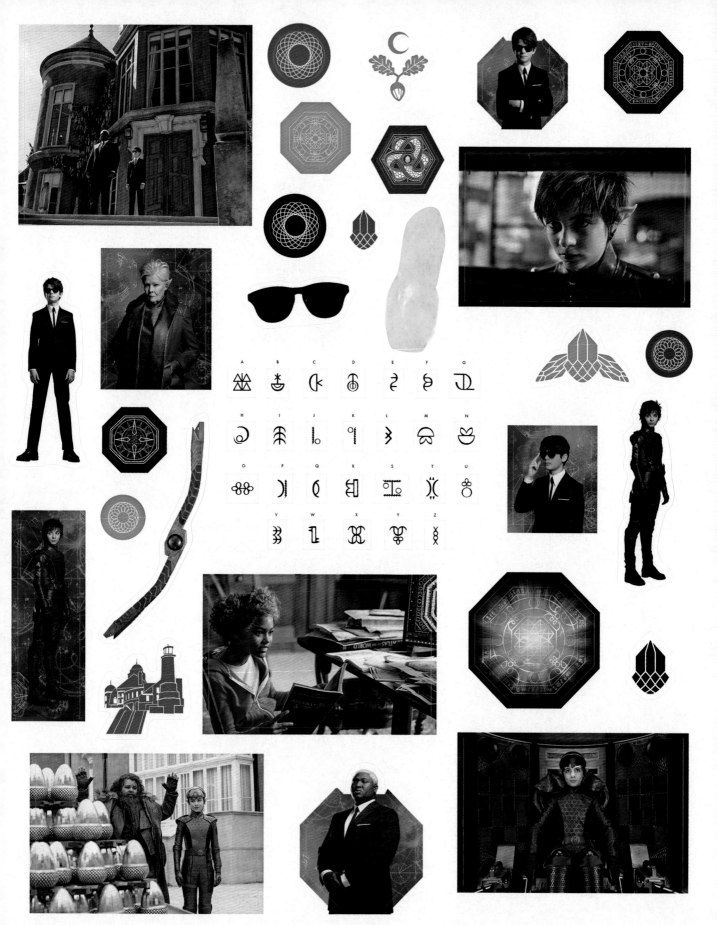

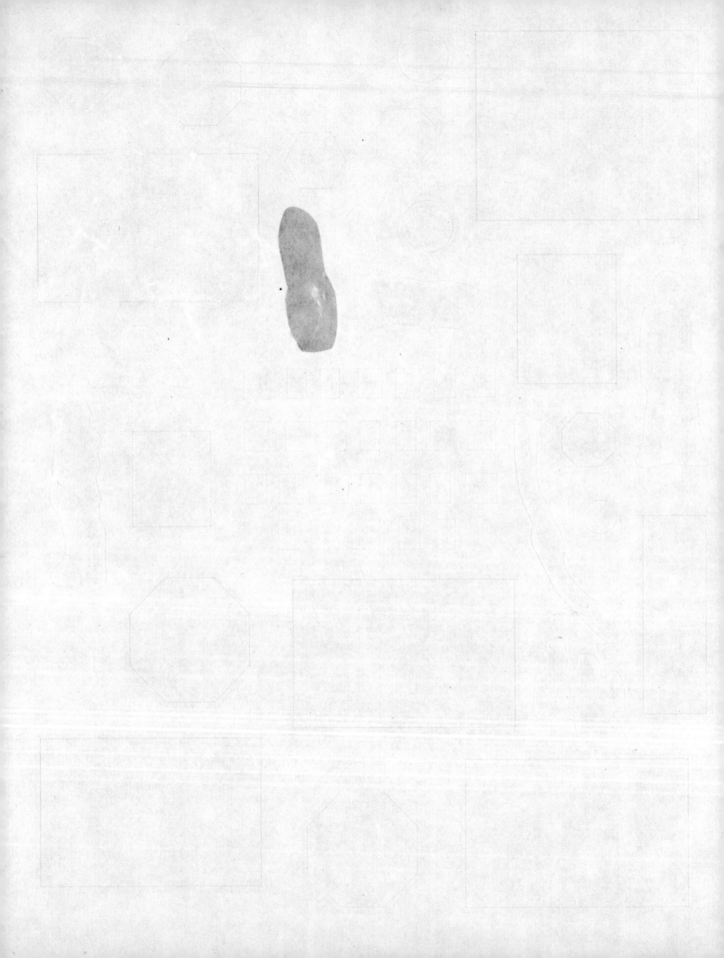